Penguin

HOW TO GIVE UP PLASTIC

WILL MCCALLUM

LEVEL

5

ADAPTED BY KAREN KOVACS
ILLUSTRATED BY GUY HARVEY
SERIES EDITOR: SORREL PITTS

The information in this book reflects the views of the author, Will McCallum, and not the views of the organization Greenpeace. So far as the author is aware the information given is correct and up to date as at March 2021.

PENGUIN BOOKS

UK | USA | Canada | Ireland | Australia
India | New Zealand | South Africa

Penguin Books is part of the Penguin Random House group of companies whose addresses can be found at global.penguinrandomhouse.com.
www.penguin.co.uk www.puffin.co.uk www.ladybird.co.uk

Penguin
Random House
UK

How to Give Up Plastic first published by Penguin Life, 2018
This Penguin Readers edition published by Penguin Books Ltd, 2021
001

Original text written by Will McCallum
Text for Penguin Readers edition adapted by Karen Kovacs
Original copyright © Will McCallum 2017
Text copyright © Penguin Books Ltd., 2021
Text design by Janette Revill
Illustrated by Guy Harvey
Illustrations copyright © Penguin Books Ltd, 2021
Cover image copyright © Penguin Books Ltd, 2020

The moral right of the original author has been asserted

Printed and bound in Great Britain by Clays Ltd, Elcograf S.p.A.

The authorized representative in the EEA is Penguin Random House Ireland, Morrison Chambers, 32 Nassau Street, Dublin D02 YH68

A CIP catalogue record for this book is available from the British Library

ISBN: 978-0-241-52074-1

All correspondence to:
Penguin Books
Penguin Random House Children's
One Embassy Gardens, 8 Viaduct Gardens,
London SW11 7BW

Contents

Note about the book

The writer, Will McCallum, is Head of Oceans at Greenpeace UK. He sees the damage that **plastic*** does in the oceans, and he often meets with **governments** and companies to ask them to use less plastic. In this book, he helps you to use less plastic, too, in your homes and in your **communities**.

You can follow Will on social media:

Twitter: @artofactivism

Instagram: @_willmccallum

Some of the information in Will's book has changed since he wrote it. Where this is true, we have changed the information so that it is correct.

Note on staying safe

In this book, you are shown how to **complain** about plastic use in shops and restaurants in your area, and in places of work or study. You are also shown how to do a beach clean and start a plastics **campaign**. Before you do these things, your parents must allow you to go and you must always take a friend or parent with you.

*Definitions of words in **bold** can be found in the glossary on pages 91–96.

Before-reading questions

1 Which of these sentences is true for you? Explain why.

   a I don't worry about how much plastic I use. I don't think
      plastic pollution is a big problem.

   b I sometimes worry about how much plastic I use.
      Maybe I should use less.

   c I try to use very little plastic. We all use too much plastic
      and it's so bad for the environment!

2 Some people say that it is bad to use too much plastic.
   Why is that, do you think? Make a list of reasons.

3 Count how many plastic things you have with you today:
   • on your body (for example, shoes, clothes, your watch);
   • in your bag (for example, your phone, credit cards);
   • on your desk (for example, pens, rubbers).
   What is your total number? Are you surprised by your total?

4 The writer of this book is Will McCallum. Read the "Note
   about the book" on page 4. What is his job?

INTRODUCTION

In the last few years, people have become extremely worried about the problem of **plastic pollution**. We read about it in newspapers, and we hear **politicians** talking about it. Famous people **encourage** us to buy **products** that are good for the environment. Tens of millions of people around the world watched *Blue Planet II*, David Attenborough's TV series. They were shocked to see a bird feeding pieces of plastic to its babies because it thought that the plastic was food. We visit our favourite beach or we walk along a river and we see plastic in the water. The problem of plastic affects us all.

When I was on a Greenpeace ship in the Antarctic, we were many hundreds of kilometres from any towns or cities, but we found tiny pieces of plastic in the ocean. I and other Greenpeace workers were sad but not shocked because we already knew that plastic is everywhere.

I have been a campaigner against plastic for years and the most common question people ask me is "What can I do to help?" *How to **Give Up** Plastic* helps you **get rid of** plastic in your own life. It also gives you information about the problem and teaches you how to encourage others – friends, family, businesses and politicians – to use less plastic.

Usually, when I talk about plastic in this book, I mean single-use plastics – that is, plastics that are used once and

scarponne

then thrown away, often taking centuries to **break down**. They include plastic bags, **straws**, coffee cups and plastic **packaging**.

We must remember that plastic is not always bad. Some people need it, for example if they are **disabled** and can only drink through a straw. But plastic is everywhere and it is a big problem for the oceans. If we continue like this there will be more plastic in the ocean than fish by 2050. So we have to do something because we all share **responsibility** for this problem. This book shows you how you can help. Each of us can make a big difference in the fight against plastic. We can use less plastic in our homes and, even more importantly, we can work with other people to try to change how our **communities** think about plastic.

We all share responsibility for this problem.

MY TOP FIVE TIPS FOR GETTING RID OF PLASTIC

1 **Go shopping.** Why am I telling you to get rid of plastic by going shopping? Because there are some things you need for a plastic-**free** life: a nice water bottle, a **reusable** coffee cup, a reusable bag for your shopping, a lunch box and some kitchen **containers**.

2 **Check what plastic you already have in your house.** Look in your bathroom, your bedroom and your kitchen. Find products with **microbeads** in and single-use plastics like cutlery (knives, forks and spoons) or straws. What should you do with them? You could send them back to the shop with a message: "In my house, we don't use single-use plastic any more."

3 **Talk to people.** Tell friends and family that you are trying to stop using plastic and encourage them to do the same.

4 **Make a plan and write it down.** Living without plastic needs planning. Which shops near you use less plastic? Can you stop buying takeaway food? This is when you buy food to take away with you and it usually comes in lots of plastic packaging. Make your own lunch instead.

5 **Start a plastic-free campaign.** Go and talk to businesses that use too much plastic, and ask your friends or a parent to join you (see note on page 4). Ask questions like "Why do you use plastic cutlery and single-use coffee cups?"

CHAPTER ONE

A short history of fighting plastic

MICROSFERIE

Banning microbeads and plastic bags

A few years ago, nobody had heard of microbeads but now people all around the world want to **ban** them. They are tiny plastic balls, less than 5mm wide, which are in many products, like **shower gel** and **toothpaste**. These microbeads go into our lakes and oceans when we wash them down the **drain**. For example, in Lake Ontario in Canada and the United States of America, there are around 1.1 million microbeads for every square kilometre. The Americans were shocked by this and they banned microbeads.

Greenpeace is famous for trying to help the environment, so in 2016, Greenpeace UK started a **petition** against microbeads. Customers were angry because they had not realized that the beads were in many of the products they used. Hundreds of thousands of people signed the petition and in 2018, microbeads were banned in the UK.

But these were not the first plastic **bans**. In 2002, Bangladesh became the first country to ban plastic bags. And since 2015, shoppers in the UK have to pay a small price for every plastic bag, which has **reduced** the number of plastic bags used by more than 95%.

Plastic bottles

Many people are angry about plastic bottles. They understand that it is silly to buy a bottle of water or **fizzy drink** and then throw the bottle away after only one use. Still, just in Britain, we use thirty-five million plastic bottles every day and less than half of those bottles are **recycled**.

Coca-Cola is the world's largest producer of plastic bottles, making over 100 billion a year. If you put all those bottles in a line, they would go around the Earth nearly 700 times. Too many of the bottles we use go into our rivers and oceans.

What can we do about this? The first thing we must do is reduce the number of them. Even the best recycling system in the world cannot recycle all our plastic **waste** because there is too much. Companies that make the bottles must find ways to help. For example, they could **produce** drinks **fountains** or bottles that customers can **refill**.

Next, there are deposit schemes – you pay a little extra for the bottle and then get that money back when you return the bottle to the shop. In Germany and Norway, where they have deposit schemes, over 90% of plastic bottles are returned and recycled.

Another thing that companies can do is increase the amount of recycled plastic in their bottles. Lots of companies now realize that they must do something to get rid of plastic, and that is great. Usually, people do not listen to campaigners but it seems that everyone is worried about plastic. If we all work together, huge changes are possible.

Taking responsibility

I started to **campaign** on plastic pollution with Greenpeace because I could see that most other campaigns made ordinary people feel guilty about how much plastic they use. But this is not fair because it is nearly impossible to stop using plastic completely. Companies are producing too much plastic; politicians are not making them take responsibility and some of the plastic in your nearest supermarket cannot be recycled. So, although we can each do something to help, ordinary people cannot take all the responsibility.

Ordinary people cannot take all the responsibility.

Sharing the responsibility between ordinary people, companies and **governments** from all countries is fair and also the only way to reduce plastic.

Who are you?

I'm Luke Massey from Greenpeace. I work to help the oceans.

Why do you care about plastic so much?

It makes me sad to see the **effects** of plastic pollution on animals. We have to stop throwing everything away and reduce our **footprint** on the Earth.

What's the best solution to the problem of plastic?

Companies that produce single-use plastic should have to pay money to the government.

What makes you most angry?

For years, businesses have produced huge amounts of plastic and not taken any responsibility. They make lots of money from making plastic, then **blame** ordinary people for throwing it away.

Do you have any top tips for getting rid of plastic?

Get a reusable water bottle and reusable coffee cup and refill them. Take a bag to the shop. Recycle as much as you can. Ask shops why they are selling so much plastic.

What is the most amazing thing that somebody has done to reduce plastic?

A man called Rob Greenfield decided to wear every piece of plastic he used in a month. Bags, containers, coffee cups, plastic bottles, everything. He went on to the streets in New York and started talking to people about plastic waste. This was amazing and it started a huge conversation in the media about plastic pollution.

CHAPTER TWO
The problem with plastic

Deep-sea plastic

Basking sharks are the second-largest fish in the world. They are huge but we do not know much about them. They are over 10 metres long but live in very deep waters. Their mouths are one metre wide, and they are always open to catch tiny animals called plankton.

I have never seen a basking shark. When I spent two months on a Greenpeace ship in Scottish seas, I hoped to see one because that is where they live. But sadly, I did not. However, we learned something about them: we now know that these fish must be eating a huge amount of microplastics – tiny pieces of plastic. The Greenpeace ship found lots of microplastics in the water.

During our time in Scotland, we also asked schools and groups to help us clean the beaches. The beaches in Scotland are often beautiful and very far from towns, but on every beach we found lots of plastic waste, including **wet wipes**, bottles and bags.

A British swimmer, Lewis Pugh, says that a few years ago, he went to Barents Island in the Arctic to do a beach clean. People have never lived there but the island's beach was covered in plastic. Some of it came from thousands of kilometres away. In less than one hour, Pugh collected a huge bag of plastic from the beach, which made him really sad. But even worse, a few days later, the beach was covered in plastic again. He wrote: "Barents Island is for polar bears, not plastic."

Even if we work really hard to get rid of plastic now and in the future, there is so much plastic already in the environment that people will be able to see it for hundreds of years.

The effect on animals

Many types of animals are affected by plastic. It is **estimated** that 90% of seabirds have plastic in their stomachs. The world's largest seabird is the albatross – its wings are 3 metres across. There is a famous photo, taken by Chris Jordan, of a dead baby albatross in the North Pacific. In the picture, its stomach is open and you can see that it is filled with plastic. Of course, the plastic killed it.

90% of seabirds have plastic in their stomachs.

It is not only animals and the environment that are affected: we are, too. Scientists in Vienna found microplastics in every human **poo** they tested.

How does plastic get into the environment?

Here are some answers to the three big questions I normally get asked.

First, how much plastic is already in the ocean? This is not an easy question to answer but it is estimated that there are 150 million **tonnes** of plastic in the ocean and that, by 2050, there will be more plastic in the ocean than fish. How can we get rid of all that plastic? We probably cannot. That is why it is important to use less plastic.

It is estimated that there are 150 million tonnes of plastic in the ocean.

Second, how much plastic enters the ocean every year? It is estimated that between 4.8 million and 12.7 million tonnes of plastic waste enter the ocean every year. That's the same as one rubbish truck every minute.

Third, where is all this plastic coming from? This is hard to answer. We think 80% comes from the land, not from ships at sea, and this is how it enters the ocean:

- Microfibres are a type of microplastic that are used to make clothes. Microfibres are washed into the ocean when we wash our clothes. About one-third of the plastic in the ocean is microfibres.
- If we drop plastic **litter**, the wind takes it into rivers and it goes into the ocean.
- If we do not recycle plastic, it can go to **landfill sites** that are by the sea and then enter the water. But even if we do try to recycle our plastic waste, scientists think that one-third escapes the world's recycling systems and enters the environment.

Microfibres are washed into the ocean when we wash our clothes. About one-third of the plastic in the ocean is microfibres.

Recycling

Every year, we produce 360 million tonnes of plastic, which is heavier than every human on Earth put together.

Only 14% of the plastic we produce is collected for recycling and 5% is actually recycled. Even countries with the best recycling systems in the world, like Japan and the Netherlands, find it impossible to recycle all plastic because there is too much. This is why it is better to produce less, not just think: "Don't worry; we can recycle it."

The waste trade

Another problem with recycling is the waste trade. This is when countries sell their waste to other countries. Millions of tonnes of plastic are moved around the world for this reason every year. You may put your plastic in the recycling bin, but then it is sold abroad, where it can be recycled but also perhaps burned. Burning plastic also damages the environment and is not the answer.

We should not always blame other countries for their plastic pollution. Some countries may not have safe drinking water, so people have to buy bottled water. And companies there may not have enough money to develop plastic-free products. The Philippines is the world's third-worst polluter of the oceans. When Greenpeace was cleaning beaches in Manila Bay in the Philippines in 2017, they collected 54,620 pieces of plastic and wrote down where the plastic came from. A lot of it had been produced by some of the world's largest and most well-known companies: Unilever, Nestlé and Procter & Gamble. So as you can see, countries in poorer parts of the world often have problems because of plastic made by companies in richer countries. It is often companies who need to take responsibility for the plastic they produce.

There is so much information about plastic that it can be hard to understand, so here are the most important **statistics**. You can use them to show your friends and family that they should use less plastic.

PLASTIC BY NUMBERS

105 billion plastic bottles are made
by Coca-Cola every year.

. . .

38 billion pieces of plastic were found on
Henderson Island in the South Pacific,
where no people live.

. . .

360 million tonnes of plastic are
produced every year.

. . .

12.7 million tonnes of plastic waste
enter the ocean every year.

. . .

500,000 pieces of plastic were found in every
square metre in a river in Manchester, UK.

. . .

450 years is how long it takes for a
plastic bottle to break down in the ocean.

. . .

90% of seabirds have plastic in their stomachs.

. . .

80% of plastic in the ocean comes from the land.

. . .

1 rubbish truck of plastic enters
the ocean every minute.

Who are you?

Tiza Mafira, Director of the Indonesia Plastic Bag Movement.

Why do you care about plastic so much?

It is a big problem in my city, Jakarta. And it is scary to think that we use many plastics only once but then they take hundreds of years to break down. Humans lived for so long without plastic so we don't need it now either.

What can people do to help?

Stop using single-use plastic. Say no every time someone tries to give you a plastic bag, straw or bottle.

What's the best solution to the problem of plastic?

Bans. They really work. Banjarmasin became the first city in Indonesia to ban plastic bags and the number of bags reduced by 80% immediately.

What changes have you made in your life to use less plastic?

I always carry a reusable bag. I say no to plastic bags, bottles, coffee cups, straws, products with microbeads and plastic food packaging. I'm a campaigner against plastic bags and tell politicians that they should try to reduce plastic.

CHAPTER THREE

Stories of hope and success

There is so much plastic entering our oceans and it seems impossible to give up all plastic, so sometimes we can lose all hope. But other people's stories can make us feel more positive. Here are some stories that I have heard.

Plastic bag bans around the world

Plastic shopping bags are a big problem around the world. Each one is normally used for only 15 minutes and scientists estimate that it will take 500–1,000 years to break down. For these reasons, it is not surprising that many countries have started to ban them. The first country that banned plastic bags was Bangladesh in 2002, and since then many other countries have done the same.

One example is Morocco. Morocco was the second-largest user of plastic bags in the world, after the United States. The country introduced a ban in 2016. Before that, Morocco used three billion plastic bags every year or 900 bags a person a year.

These bag bans are already reducing how much plastic enters the oceans.

Other single-use plastic bans

In some places, governments want to ban more than just plastic bags. San Francisco has banned plastic bottles and other types of plastic, too. One part of India, Karnataka, has done even more. They have banned all single-use plastics, including bags and cutlery. Antigua and Barbuda have banned plastic food containers and the European Union has decided to ban single-use plastics including straws and cutlery.

These examples show us that politicians know that we must reduce our plastic use. And bans are a very good way of achieving that.

193 countries admit that there is a problem

In 2017, 193 countries met in Nairobi to discuss the problem of plastic. At the end of the meeting, they agreed that action was needed. This is amazing because it is difficult for 193 different countries to agree on anything. Thirty-nine of those countries also agreed to reduce plastic entering the ocean.

People going plastic-free

Lots of people are trying to reduce their plastic use. Whole families are trying to live without plastic for one week and over two million people in 150 countries have tried to have a "Plastic-Free July", one month without plastic. A plastic-free life might not be possible for most people. However, lots of us are trying our best. Some people talk or write about what they are doing online. If you have a question that this book does not answer, I am sure that you can find the answer online in **blogs**, in Instagram posts and on Facebook pages.

Plastic-free blogs

This book has plenty of **tips** for reducing your plastic use but if you ever need more information, look at these amazing blogs. They have lots of good advice.

Plastic-Free July

Around the world, people are trying to live with less plastic in July. This blog has interesting stories, advice and ideas. Will you try a plastic-free July?

www.plasticfreejuly.org

Beth Terry – My Plastic-Free Life

Beth's blog has an amazing 100 Steps to a Plastic-Free Life so you can start living life without plastic. It also asks you to take photos of your plastic waste for one week so that you can see how much plastic you use.

myplasticfreelife.com

Anne Marie – The Zero-Waste Chef

Anne Marie gives you plenty of tips for going plastic-free in the kitchen.

zerowastechef.com

It is easier to reduce plastic if we all share our ideas with each other. I would love to hear how you are reducing plastic. Share your ideas with us at:

#BreakFreeFromPlastic

Who are you?

I'm Louise Edge and I'm an oceans campaigner at Greenpeace.

Why do you care about plastic so much?

I see how badly plastic is **polluting** our world. It is everywhere – in rivers, in Arctic ice – and all animals eat plastic. Tiny plankton eat it and the biggest fish eat it. And we are eating it, too. That can't be good for our bodies.

What can people do to help?

We can make lots of small changes in our own lives. However, it is big companies and governments who can make the biggest difference by reducing their use of plastic packaging. We must tell them that we want change – on social media (Twitter, Instagram, TikTok, etc.) or when we visit a shop or meet politicians.

What's the worst example of plastic pollution you've seen?

I visited Freedom Island, a home for birds in Manila Bay. The whole beach was covered in plastic packaging. In the sea, I saw plastic waste next to dead fish and seabirds. It made me really sad. With some other people I cleaned the beach but the next day, there was more plastic waste. I realized that plastic packaging is a big problem and that we need the help of big companies like Nestlé and Unilever. They make the packaging, and they must help with the problem.

Do you have any top tips for getting rid of plastic?

I carry a reusable water bottle and cup, and I reuse shopping bags. I also now use **solid soap**, shower gel and **shampoo** because the solid products don't need plastic packaging.

What makes it difficult to get rid of plastic?

Producing plastic makes a lot of money for big companies like Exxon Mobil and Shell so they don't want to stop doing it. But lots of people want them to reduce plastic – so they have to change.

What is the most amazing thing that somebody has done to reduce plastic?

In Manila, a community of people are trying not to throw away any plastic. There were mountains of bin bags in their streets, and they decided to do something. Now they reuse or recycle most of their plastic and the whole area only sends four rubbish bags to landfill every day. Most of that is **nappies** and all the rest is reused or recycled – amazing!

CHAPTER FOUR

How can one person make a difference?

Every story of success against plastic begins with one person or a small group of people who take action. You can see that from the stories in this book. It is hard to imagine that one person can make a difference – but you really can. You may only reduce your plastic use by one bottle today and a coffee cup the next day, but you are showing other people what is possible.

Every story of success against plastic begins with one person or a small group of people who take action.

The changes we make in our own lives can have a big effect on others, so you must tell people what you are doing and why. Do not forget: politicians and company directors are just people, like you or me. If they hear our stories about reducing our plastic use, they may be encouraged to make changes, too. Everybody has a family and friends – and modern technology helps us talk or write to them more easily than ever. So talk about what you are doing. Tell your family and friends about getting rid of plastic. They may follow you!

HOW TO GIVE UP PLASTIC: A PROMISE

Do you like some of the people and campaigns that you have read about in this book so far? Then before you read the rest of the book, make this promise to yourself. From today, I promise that I will do my best to give up plastic, although it will not be easy or quick, and sometimes it may not be possible. I promise to:

- **say no to plastic when I can, for example not using plastic straws, bags, coffee cups or bottles;**
- **reduce my plastic footprint when I can by choosing products not made of plastic;**
- **reuse plastic products, like containers, if I cannot say no to them or reduce my use of them;**
- **recycle or reuse everything that I can;**
- **tell everyone I know about how I am getting rid of plastic and encourage them to join me!**

Signed ....

Date ....

#BreakFreeFromPlastic

Who are you?

We are sisters Amy and Ella Meek. We started a campaign group called Kids Against Plastic. We are often on the news talking about reducing plastic.

Why do you care about plastic so much?

We are kids now but we know that, when we are adults, the problem of plastic will be our problem. Since we started Kids Against Plastic, we've picked up 100,000 pieces of the Big 4 plastic products (single-use cups, straws, bottles and bags). We've also encouraged many cafés, businesses and schools to become Plastic Clever – that means using less single-use plastic and more reusable plastic. We tell other people about plastic as much as we can, giving talks (for example on TEDx), talking in schools and starting new Kids Against Plastic groups around the country.

What can people do to help?

Become Plastic Clever! Reduce your use of plastic cups, straws, bottles and bags.

What's the worst example of plastic pollution you've seen?

In a village called Arrochar in Scotland, we saw a horrible amount of plastic on the beach. It has a big effect on the people who live there but they produced none of it. They clean the beach every month but more plastic comes.

What's the best solution to the problem of plastic?

Using reusable products. It can also save you money because most cafés now give you a **discount** for using a reusable cup! And we should reduce our use of bottled water because in many countries the water is safe so you don't need to buy plastic water bottles!

What changes have you made in your life to use less plastic?

We don't use single-use plastic, most importantly the Big 4 (cups, straws, bottles and bags).

What makes you most angry?

Plastic packaging on products that don't need packaging! For example, why do companies sell fruit and vegetables in plastic?

Do you have any top tips for getting rid of plastic?

Start by doing something small! Say no to single-use plastic – that can have a bigger effect than you can imagine.

What makes it difficult to get rid of plastic?

We all use too much plastic packaging. It's everywhere, and it's difficult to stop using it.

Giving up plastic at home

Now you know why we should get rid of plastic, so you are ready for the next part of the book. The next few chapters show you lots of ways to reduce your plastic footprint. But first, a top tip – go slowly and make new changes every week. The best place to start is in the bathroom . . .

CHAPTER FIVE

Giving up plastic in the bathroom

Look in your bathroom cupboard or next to your bath and you can probably see lots of plastic containers. They will all soon be thrown away. Let's look at how to get rid of some of these plastic products.

Refillables

Things like shampoos and hand creams usually come in small plastic containers that are used and then thrown away. But more and more of us want to get rid of plastic,  so what can we do? We can buy **refillables**. This is when you buy, for example, five or ten litres of shampoo in a large container and refill the small bottle of shampoo from this container when the bottle is empty. This uses less plastic. Some shops will also refill bottles for you. And the small bottle does not have to be plastic: you can use a glass one.

Solid products

If you cannot find large containers of bathroom products or shops that can refill your small bottles for you, then you can use solid soap, shower gel, shampoo and **deodorant** instead. Be sure that they do not use plastic packaging. Look online or in some shops, like Lush.

Sponges

Doctors say that it is better to wash without a **sponge** because they get dirty easily. If you really want to use a sponge, try a natural one called a loofah, a kind of dried fruit.

Do not use microbeads

A few years ago, nobody had heard of microbeads but now governments all over the world are banning them. They can be found in toothpaste, sun cream, **make-up** and hand wash.

If your country has not yet banned microbeads, be careful when you buy products because microbeads are washed down the drain and pollute our oceans. You can find the names of companies that do not use microbeads on **www.beatthemicrobead.org**. If you want to see whether products you already own have microbeads in, check for these words on the packaging:

- Polyethylene (PE)
- Polypropylene (PP)
- Polyethylene terephthalate (PET)
- Polymethyl methacrylate (PMMA)
- Polytetrafluoroethylene (PTFE)
- Nylon

If you already own a product with microbeads in, then how about sending it back to the company that made it and asking for your money back? They might not give you your money back but at least they will know you are not happy that they are using microbeads.

Cotton buds

 A short time after the microbeads ban, several countries, including Scotland and France, banned cotton buds with plastic in them. Cotton buds are used to clean your cars or take off make-up. When Waitrose (a UK supermarket group) banned them, it saved twenty-one tonnes of plastic – that is a lot for such a tiny product!

If you cannot imagine life without ear buds, try ones made from wood or paper. The company Johnson & Johnson has promised to stop using plastic in their cotton buds. Call them and ask when they are going to introduce this change in your country.

Make-up

Make-up is a problem because nearly all make-up is sold in plastic packaging. Write to the producer of your favourite make-up and tell them to stop using plastic.

Taking off make-up is not a problem, however. To take off your make-up, you do not need to buy single-use **pads**, which come in plastic packaging and are often made with plastic. Instead, go plastic-free with reusable cotton pads made by Sinplástico or a konjac sponge made from vegetables.

Brushing your teeth

It is difficult not to use plastic when brushing your teeth. There could be microbeads in your toothpaste and it comes in plastic packaging, and your toothbrush is made from plastic. But there are some things you can do. Truthpaste and Georganics sell toothpaste in glass containers. Or you can make your own tooth **powder**. Do not worry! It still keeps your teeth clean and has been used for centuries. Go to this website and search for "dentist approved tooth powder" to find out how to make it:

www.goingzerowaste.com ✸

Getting rid of hair

You want to get rid of plastic but you probably also want to get rid of hair on your body! Do not buy single-use razors or razors you throw away after a few uses. Buy a safety razor. It might seem scary at first but they work well. Many shops still sell them.

Tampons

Women's **tampons** and pads have plastic in them. One pad has as much plastic as four plastic bags. Women use between 12,000 and 16,000 tampons in their lives, and used tampons are often found on beaches.

An easy **solution** is to buy tampons without plastic, like those from Natracare. Remember: do not put tampons down the toilet, even ones made without plastic. They are often later found in the oceans and on beaches.

You can also buy a cup from a company like Mooncup. A cup is more expensive than a tampon but you only need one and you can safely reuse it for years.

Down the toilet

Tampons are not the only things that are put down the toilet. Wet wipes are often put down the toilet, too, and later found on beaches. Wet wipes are made using plastic and have plastic packaging. If you must use them to take off your make-up put them in the bin, not down the toilet!

Toilet paper is made of paper but it comes in plastic packaging. Some companies, for example Who Gives a Crap and Ecoleaf, use paper packaging, and they send you a large amount of toilet paper at one time, which is better for the environment.

The toilet brush that you use to clean your toilet is probably plastic. You can buy a plastic-free one from a company like Boobalou.

You have looked in your bathroom now, so how about completing a plastic-free plan? Write down the plastic-free products that you or your parents will buy or the changes that you or your parents will make to use less plastic. Take a photo of your plan and share it online so that others can join you!

. ECOLEAF .

The bathroom

Plastic-free plan

Shampoo ....

Soap ....

Hand wash ....

Shaving cream ....

Razor ....

Deodorant ....

Sponge ....

Make-up ....

Taking off make-up ....

Toothbrush ....

Toothpaste ....

Tampons ....

Toilet paper ....

Toilet brush ....

Other products ....

Giving up plastic in the bedroom

Microfibres and clothes

It is a surprise for most people that the clothes they wear produce a lot of the plastic in the ocean. Tiny pieces of your clothes, normally made from plastic **materials** such as polyester, come off every time you wear or wash them or when you throw them away. Polyester is cheap and easy to use, and it is in 60% of our clothes. It is estimated that seventy-four million tonnes of plastic were produced for clothes in 2018.

More than one-third of the plastic in the ocean comes from our clothes when we wash them. The microfibres in clothes are so small that they wash into the drain from our washing machines. From just one fleece jacket, a type of warm jacket made from plastic, 250,000 microfibres can be washed into the ocean.

But if these microfibres are so small, how can they damage the ocean? Although we cannot see them, they look like food to plankton. Next, bigger sea animals eat the plankton and the plastic enters their bodies. Then, even bigger animals eat those animals and the plastic enters their bodies – and it continues like that. In the end, the plastic could even be found on your dinner plate, in the fish you eat.

So what can you do? If microfibres are used so much, a solution is hard to imagine. Here are a few things you can do.

Coronavirus

Products that people use to stop themselves from catching coronavirus are producing lots of plastic waste. A reusable face mask made of a natural material like cotton can be as useful as a single-use plastic one, if you wash it correctly.

Shopping

Buy fewer clothes

Reduce how many clothes you buy, fix your old clothes and, even if the fashion changes, keep your clothes from last year. It will help the environment and save you money at the same time!

Buy fewer new clothes

Next time you go shopping, look for shops that sell second-hand (already used) clothes. And you can buy clothes made from recycled plastic.

Buy fewer clothes made from plastic

Try to buy clothes made of natural materials like wool and cotton. Sadly, clothes made of these materials are often more expensive, but they last a long time.

Complain

In Chapter Eleven, I will give you more information on how to campaign but here's a good tip. If you are in a shop, looking for clothes made of natural materials and all the clothes are made of plastic, then tell the shop that you are not happy about it! You can talk to the shop manager or write an email or go on social media. The more people who **complain**, the more these shops will listen to us.

Washing

Do you need to wash that?

Only wash clothes made of plastic when you have to. Think: can I wear this again before I wash it?

Wash your clothes smarter

Wash your clothes like this to reduce the number of microfibres that go down the drain:

- Use a cold wash or at least the coldest wash you can.
- Fill the washing machine.
- Wash clothes for a shorter amount of time.

Bedding

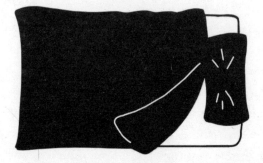

Of course, clothes are not the only material in the bedroom. There are also curtains, for example, but we do not wash those very often. With **bedding**, do the same thing that you do with clothes: be sure that your bedding is made of natural materials like cotton. You can even buy bedding made of recycled plastic that feels like wool.

The bedroom

Plastic-free plan

Clothes – materials ....

Clothes – how many you buy ....

Clothes – second-hand ....

Face masks ....

Washing clothes ....

Bedding ....

CHAPTER SEVEN

Giving up plastic in the kitchen

Of all the plastic we buy, nearly half of it is packaging. If you speak to any of the big supermarkets about reducing plastic packaging, you often hear the same thing: without plastic packaging, there would be 40% more food waste. They say that this is because, without plastic packaging, food is more easily damaged. But this is not true. A report by Friends of the Earth found that as plastic packaging has increased, food waste has increased, too. Food waste in European homes doubled between 2004 and 2014, while plastic packaging increased by more than 25%.

The report also found that packaging looks nice and makes people buy more food. Then they have too much food so they throw some of it away.

Often supermarkets do not want to change, but if lots of us tell them that we are not happy they will listen. In the UK, Iceland supermarkets have promised to be plastic-free by 2023. So write to your supermarket if you think they use too much plastic packaging on their products.

Until all supermarkets stop selling plastic, here are some ideas to reduce the plastic in your kitchen.

Going shopping
What do you need?
Before you go to the supermarket, write down what you

need to buy. If you do not, you will probably buy extra things that you do not need.

Reusable bags
Check before you leave the house: do you have your reusable bags? Over 500 billion plastic bags are used every year around the world – that is at least one million every minute – but using a reusable bag instead of a plastic one is very easy.

Where to shop
Continue going to your favourite shop
You could continue going to your favourite shop or supermarket to buy food while trying not to buy products with too much plastic packaging. You could also tell the shop if you think they should reduce their plastic footprint. For example, speak to the manager in the shop or on the phone (see note on page 4). Or take a photo of the packaging and post the photo on social media.

Using social media

An easy way to show that you are angry about plastic packaging is to post a photo of it on social media, for example Instagram, Twitter or Snapchat. Remember to **tag** the shop or the company that makes the product and, also, remember to use this hashtag:

#BreakFreeFromPlastic

Everyone can remember a time when they were extremely angry because a product had too much plastic packaging. In 2018, the UK supermarket Marks & Spencer was selling a vegetable product with too much plastic packaging. A shopper posted a photo of it on Twitter and lots of people were shocked and angry. As a result, Marks & Spencer stopped selling that product. So if you see a product with lots of plastic packaging, share it with your friends and family online. You might make some of these companies change their stupid packaging.

Many supermarkets do also sell fruit and vegetables with no packaging at all. Always choose these if you can.

Do not shop in supermarkets
It is also possible not to shop in supermarkets. Markets and smaller shops like butchers and bakers usually do not use as much plastic. You can put the products into a paper bag or reusable bag, or take along your own container.

Maybe you do not have a small shop near your house or maybe it is too expensive. If that is true for you, try buying online. Some companies, like Riverford in the UK or Isarland Ökokiste in Germany, bring fruit and vegetable boxes to your door and use very little plastic packaging.

What to buy
Fresh food
What should you buy to reduce your plastic footprint? Making your shopping completely plastic-free is not possible

for everyone. You might not live near the right shops or you might not have enough time to look for plastic-free products. But there are still things that you can do. Buying food that is fresh is the easiest way to reduce your plastic use because it is often sold without plastic packaging.

Make your own

If you like cooking, do not buy **snacks** – buy fresh food and make your own snacks. Snacks that you buy, like chocolate, produce a lot of plastic waste. Look online for ideas for snacks that you can make at home.

No unrecyclable plastic

Some types of plastic can be recycled and some types cannot. Check which types can be recycled in your area and do not buy plastic that you cannot recycle.

More supermarkets should stop selling food in plastic packaging that cannot be recycled but so far, most have not. Black plastic cannot be recycled so it is burned or goes to landfill instead. If your favourite food comes in black plastic, complain to the company that makes it.

If you do buy food in plastic packaging, look for the recycling symbol and only buy products with this symbol.

You can recycle different types of plastic in different cities and countries, so go online and check what you can recycle where you live.

Drinks

Teabags

Some companies use plastic in their teabags. After 200,000 people signed a petition to Unilever, the company that owns the tea producer PG Tips, they promised to get rid of plastic. If the packaging for your favourite tea does not say that it is plastic-free, look online. If you cannot find the answer there, call or email them or send them a message on Twitter to check. You could also start buying tea in boxes, not in little teabags.

Milk

In many places around the world, milk is still sold in glass bottles. These are returned after use, washed and used again. Can you buy milk in glass bottles in your area? If you live near a farm, can they refill your bottles with milk for you?

Cooking and cleaning

If possible, keep food in glass containers, not plastic ones. Try not to use single-use plastic **wrap** to cover food. Buy big containers of washing-up liquid, etc. and refill the smaller bottle. Ecover is a great company – you can refill your old containers with their products in some shops and the company's packaging is mostly recycled plastic.

For cleaning your kitchen you can use loofahs, like in your bathroom. These are natural sponges. Do not buy single-use wet wipes. Instead, find **cloths** made from natural materials like cotton or wool, and then wash and reuse them.

If you want more advice for the kitchen, the Zero-Waste Chef, Anne Marie, has a lot of information on her website. You can find ideas for making your own food using products with no plastic packaging. If you do not like cooking or if you eat a lot of takeaways, then speak to your favourite takeaway restaurant and ask them to stop using plastic packaging.

You have looked in your kitchen now, so how about completing a plastic-free plan? Write down the plastic-free products that you or your parents will buy or the changes that you or your parents will make to use less plastic. Take a photo of your plan and share it online so others can join you!

The kitchen

Plastic-free plan

Plastic bags ....

Fresh fruit and vegetables ....

Meat and fish ....

Milk products ....

Snacks ....

Tea and coffee ....

Food containers ....

Washing-up liquid ....

Sponges and cloths ....

Takeaways ....

Other products that you often buy ....

Who are you?

My name is Bonnie Wright. I'm an oceans campaigner and an actor.

Why do you care about plastic so much?

I surf and I'm often in the water, so I see plastic pollution a lot. Here in Los Angeles, and also in other places that I visit, there is not a good recycling system so people cannot easily recycle. Plastic is easy, so more and more people are using it. When I look in the water and I see plastic, I know it is going to be there forever. It doesn't break down and that idea really shocks me. But we can all do something about it.

What's the worst example of plastic pollution you've seen?

I was on a Greenpeace ship between the Bahamas and Miami. The water looked so beautiful and blue but after just one hour, we found lots of pieces of plastic. There is no sea or ocean without plastic and that is so sad.

What makes you most angry?

Why do we need plastic packaging for fruit? Fruit already has a natural skin, which stops the fruit from being damaged.

What makes it difficult to get rid of plastic?

We might be able to choose to use a recyclable cup or reusable bag but many people in the world can't. Maybe they can't buy them in their area or they don't have any money to buy them. So we need to complain to companies and tell them to change. If lots of people complain, companies will change because they don't want to lose customers.

What other changes have you made in your life to use less plastic?

I'm slowly starting to get rid of plastic in my house but it's hard and it takes time. My favourite things are reusable – for example, fruit and vegetable bags made of cloth. I always have my reusable cup for tea, coffee or water. I found a company that sends you shampoo in the post and you send back the metal containers.

Do you have any other message for people?

Plastic is a really big problem but small changes make a difference. It can be hard, so choose one area of your house – for example, food or cleaning products or bathroom products – and start there. Be polite but don't be afraid to talk to your nearest restaurant or coffee shop about their use of plastic (see note on page 4). Or maybe ask them to give a discount if people bring their own reusable cup. It is important to talk to businesses and changes are happening.

"

CHAPTER EIGHT

Giving up plastic outside the home

Walking down the street, you can usually see lots of litter. Our lives are fast and busy, we have no time to stop and enjoy the moment, and the litter that we leave shows this. I will show you in this chapter how to reduce the amount of plastic you buy outside your home.

If you go out and forget your plastic-free cup or container but you really want a coffee or snack, do not feel guilty. Even if you forget for one whole week, there are still fifty-one weeks of the year when you are not using plastic – and that is amazing. If you really want to get rid of plastic, there are plenty of quick and easy ways to reduce your plastic use outside the home.

Plastic bottles

About 500 billion plastic bottles are sold every year – that's 20,000 a second! If you put them in a line, they would reach halfway to the sun. In the past we did not use plastic bottles; we used glass ones. In some parts of the world, like Africa and Latin America, glass bottles are often still used, for example for milk or juice. They should continue to do this and not start using plastic instead.

We must remember that plastic has made life easier for many people. Perhaps they cannot drink easily without a straw or perhaps their water is not safe to drink. Before we get angry with a stranger or country because they are using plastic, we must think about their reasons. Here is Jamie Szymkowiak, a campaigner for disabled people.

As so many people are now against plastic straws, many places like restaurants, cinemas and sports centres have stopped using straws or are now using metal or paper straws instead. But we must think about the effects of a straw ban on disabled people.

Plastic straws are cheap and can be used for drinking hot and cold drinks. Some disabled people need them. For example, perhaps they can only drink very slowly – paper straws go soft quite quickly. Or perhaps they can't hold a spoon so they need a straw to drink soup – most plastic-free straws can't be used over 40°C.

What can we do?

I'm part of a disabilities group called One in Five. We are asking companies to produce a plastic-free straw that can be used with hot and cold drinks.

Of course, disabled people agree that we all need to reduce single-use plastics. Everyone must work together to ask companies to find a solution that is good for everyone, including disabled people.

Reusable bottles

Buying a good reusable water bottle may be the most important thing that you do to get rid of plastic in your life. In Chapter Eleven, you will find advice on campaigning for more water fountains in your area and on encouraging cafés and restaurants to let you refill your bottle. However, if you buy a bottle of water every day, then just refill your reusable bottle every morning at home and you will already reduce your plastic footprint by 365 bottles a year. It is true that some places do not let you refill your bottle. If they do not let you, tell them that you will go online and tell people that they are polluting the oceans (see note on page 4).

If you think metal water bottles are ugly, do not worry. There are many types of reusable bottles you can buy and you will be able to find pretty or cool ones.

Soda makers

Just in the United States, over 1,500 plastic bottles are used every second so, as you can see, we need to find more ways to reduce our use of them. One way is to buy a machine for your home that makes fizzy drinks, called a soda maker. There are many types and you can find them on **www.sodamakerclub.com**.

In the United States, over 1,500 plastic bottles are used every second.

When you can only choose single-use plastic

We have all bought a single-use bottle and then thrown it away. If you cannot choose to use a soda maker or refillable bottle, then do these things instead:

1. Choose a drink in a container that can be recycled easily, like cardboard, a can or a glass bottle. This is the best solution if you forget your reusable bottle or cannot buy one.

2. Pick a drink from a company that uses more recycled plastic in their bottles. Some companies, like Naked Juice and Resource water, use 100% recycled plastic in their bottles. Do not worry if the plastic is not clear – this is because recycled plastic is never completely clear. Companies must not use this as a reason not to use recycled plastic.

3. Choose a drinks bottle made from 100% recyclable plastic. If you cannot find a drink in cardboard, a can or a glass bottle and you cannot find a bottle made from recycled plastic, then at least choose one made from recyclable plastic. Companies should not make bottles from plastic that cannot be recycled. Most big companies are promising to make bottles from 100% recyclable plastic within the next few years. Why do we have to wait when they are making huge numbers of bottles every year?

Finally, if you do buy a plastic bottle, do not drop it as litter. If you can, take it home and put it in your recycling bin. If you are lucky and you live in an area with a deposit scheme, then use it. A deposit scheme is where you pay a little extra for the bottle and then get that money back when you return the bottle to the shop. These schemes are a very good way of reducing the number of bottles that enter the environment.

Coffee cups

We see it everywhere – people going to work, school or college with a coffee cup in their hand. Most of them do not realize there is a problem with these cups. Even I thought they were all right. But they are not. They are made of **cardboard** but inside there is also thin plastic. For this reason, most of them are not recyclable. Of the 2.5 billion coffee cups that British people use every year, only 0.25% are recycled. Starbucks uses over four billion coffee cups a year and it is not doing much to reduce this huge number.

Of the 2.5 billion coffee cups that British people use every year, only 0.25% are recycled.

The easiest way to give up plastic coffee cups is to get a reusable cup. You can buy them in different sizes and colours and some are not very expensive. The most famous producer is KeepCup. They have sold millions of cups in ovcr thirty countries. Many coffee shops give you a discount if you bring your own cup, so you could save money as well. Shops may try to give you a little plastic spoon but do not take it. Ask for a metal spoon instead. Or you can carry a metal spoon with you to use when you are out.

Cutlery

Plastic cutlery, often in its own plastic bag, has become a part of normal life outside the home. Even worse, most of the time we only use the fork and not the spoon or  knife. Carrying your own cutlery with you (perhaps just a fork) and saying no to plastic cutlery are great ways to reduce your plastic footprint. Either take cutlery from your kitchen or buy smaller cutlery from a camping shop or online. If you really need a fork, knife and spoon, buy a Spork, which is all three in one. If you use chopsticks instead, keep the last plastic ones you are given and reuse them.

Plastic bags

We should completely stop using plastic bags. They make problems for our cities and kill animals. Plastic bags are probably the most used single-use plastic product in the world. More and more countries are realizing that they are a bad idea and I am sure that other countries will follow them soon. You probably already have reusable bags or you can easily find some. If you prefer, you can take cardboard boxes from the supermarket for your shopping.

Straws

There is a YouTube video of a plastic straw being painfully taken out of a **turtle**'s nose. This shocked people and many more people now know about the problem of plastic straws. As we said, some people need them, but the rest of us should not use them. When you order a drink at a bar or in a restaurant, remember to say that you do not want a straw. If you really like using a straw, then buy a reusable one online and take it with you.

How about completing the plastic-free plan below? Write down the plastic-free products that you or your parents will buy or the changes that you or your parents will make to use less plastic. Take a photo of your plan and share it online so others can join you!

Outside the home

Plastic-free plan

Plastic bottles ....

Coffee cups ....

Cutlery ....

Plastic bags ....

Straws ....

Other ....

CHAPTER NINE

Giving up plastic in kids' rooms

Here is how to make some changes, so that your family can reduce its plastic footprint.

Nappies

Just in the United States, an estimated 27.4 billion nappies are used every year, and 90% of them go to landfill where they will take over 500 years to break down. For the baby in the family, your parents could choose reusable cloth nappies instead, for example from the company Bambino Mio.

Toys and sports

Here are some ideas for reducing plastic when playing sports or with toys.

• Buy second-hand (already used) toys and sports products. Look on websites like eBay or in second-hand shops for things that are not new. Then, when you are bored of them, you can sell them or give them to someone.

• Buy recycled plastic or go plastic-free. Bureo sells skateboards made from recycled ocean plastic, for example.

Parties

Glitter

Glitter is beautiful but it is made of thousands of pieces of plastic and is washed down the drain or taken away by the wind. You can find plastic-free glitter, for example from Lush and Eco Glitter Fun.

Make your own plastic-free decorations

Explore websites like Pinterest or Instructables, which show you how to make beautiful plastic-free **decorations**. Here are four ideas for a plastic-free party:

- Make decorations from old material.
- Make pom-poms, which are balls made using wool and a cardboard circle.
- Get a reusable material "Happy Birthday" decoration.
- Ask friends to help you wash up after the party so you do not need to use single-use cups, plates and cutlery.

Everyone goes plastic-free

Tell your friends that you should *all* have birthday parties that are better for the environment this year. For example, buy just one box of decorations and share them.

Wrap less

Lots of the **wrapping paper** we use has plastic on it so it cannot be recycled. Buy paper that has no plastic, reuse old wrapping paper or do not wrap the present – 50% of people say that they prefer getting an **unwrapped** present to a present that is wrapped in plastic wrapping paper.

There are many other ways of reducing the plastic in your life. I recommend exploring blogs like Life Without Plastic.

Now you can complete the plastic-free plan below. Write down the plastic-free products that you or your parents will buy or the changes that you or your parents will make to use less plastic. Take a photo of your plan and share it online so others can join you!

Kids' rooms

Plastic-free plan

Nappies ....

Glitter ....

Toys ....

Sports products ....

Party decorations ....

Wrapping paper ....

Other ....

CHAPTER TEN
Giving up plastic at work or school

It is possible to make big changes at work, school or university. This is because you see the people you work or study with every day so they cannot escape you! You can also encourage your parents to campaign in their workplace. This chapter gives you some ideas for giving up plastic in your work or studies.

Change other people

Talk to people about what you have learned in this book, give them a few statistics or send them a news story from the internet about plastic use. Then they can join you in giving up plastic.

If you want to do more – you will need to campaign. Where you work or study, put up a **poster** about plastic pollution or send everyone an email about it. Start by encouraging people to give up the top five products: plastic bags, bottles, coffee cups, straws and cutlery.

Be careful: do not be too negative when you talk to them. Be gentle and positive. Instead of telling people what to do – for example, "You mustn't use straws" – try using questions like "Do you want to learn how to give up plastic?" That way, you will encourage people to talk to you and ask questions.

Get plastic-free products

Your place of study or your parents' office may be very big. You could ask businesses to give you a discount if you buy a large number of their plastic-free products for everyone. Or, if you are starting a plastic-free campaign, can your manager or director help you by, for example, giving a free reusable water bottle to everyone? If they do this, they will have less rubbish to throw away because their workers or students will not use single-use water bottles any more.

Give a talk

A talk, at lunchtime or during lessons, given by a plastics campaigner can get people interested in giving up plastic. Search online for groups near you who are campaigning against plastics, like Greenpeace or Friends of the Earth. I am sure that a campaigner would be very happy to come and talk to people at your school or workplace.

Plastic-free competition

Have a friendly competition with another class or group. One day a week or one month a year, have a competition to see which class or group can produce the least plastic waste. And why not have a plastic-free lunch together – everyone can bring something to share? Then, during the lunch, you can discuss how to make your place of study or work start giving up plastic.

Make big changes

Walk around your place of study or work, or your parents' work, and find all the single-use plastic in use. Is there any plastic cutlery? Are there only plastic cups at the water fountain? Write down what you see. Maybe you can take the manager or some friends with you on your walk. Ask the manager or director, "Why have you chosen to use plastic here? Is it because it's easy or cheap?" If they do not want to change, show them some plastic-free ideas from this book.

If they still do not listen, then you need to start a campaign. Start a petition and ask your friends to sign it. If the manager can see that you have good ideas for going plastic-free, and also that lots of other people agree with you, then they will probably listen to you.

Become famous

Finally, if a place of study or work starts to become plastic-free, think about ways to make them famous for it! Your company or school could post on social media or make a poster so that customers or future students can see the changes that they have made.

CHAPTER ELEVEN

Giving up plastic in your community

This chapter shows you how to be part of a bigger change, in your area, in your country or around the world. We need to work together so that important people listen to us.

Do not forget, when you read this chapter, that your own experience is very important. You can use this book or search online for the answers to difficult questions or the right statistics, but the best way to encourage other people is to tell them a story from your heart.

Where to start

Find a group in your area that campaigns on plastic. Look for posters in your nearest café or search online. The group should be interested in reducing all plastics, not just picking up litter.

However, of course it is good to pick up litter. To help you do your own beach clean, here is some information from the Marine Conservation Society (MCS), a group that cleans beaches in the UK. If there is no beach near you, change some of the advice and clean your nearest park instead. If you have any questions, go to the MCS website: **www.mcsuk.org/beachwatch**.

PLANNING YOUR BEACH CLEAN

Before the day

1. Find a beach and check online to see if there is already a group that do beach cleans there.

2. Check when the **tide** is high. The best time to do a beach clean is four hours after high tide. This means the tide will be going out during your beach clean, not coming in, which could be dangerous.

3. Ask the owner of the beach if it is OK to do a beach clean.

4. Ask the owner where you should leave the extra rubbish that you collect.

5. Check whether there are any dangers on the beach. The MCS website has tips for this, or ask the beach owner if there is anything dangerous. Visit the beach before the event to check whether it looks safe.

6. Make some posters. You can even do a press release (a report for a newspaper about an event) for the newspaper in your area or city (see page 75-78 for advice on writing a press release). The MCS website has lots of tips.

7. Get other people to join you by using a Google form. Email people about a week before the event to tell them what to bring: the right clothes and shoes, water, food, sun cream, thick/gardening gloves (but not plastic ones!). Also tell them where to meet you.

You are ready for the big day!

On the day

Things to bring:

☐ Your notes on any dangers on the beach.

☐ Pens and paper so that everyone can write the types and amount of litter that they collect.

☐ Bin bags!

☐ Things to help you clean the beach, for example thick/gardening gloves (but not plastic ones).

☐ Something to weigh your rubbish at the end (find the total number of kilograms).

☐ A **First Aid Kit** (somebody may hurt themselves) and a container for collecting glass or other things that can cut you.

☐ A **survey** form. Use the form from the MCS website, changing some parts if you need to.

☐ Letters from the parents of people under 16, which say that they allow their child to come on the beach clean.

Arrive at the beach before the event starts so that you can check for any dangers. Choose a 100-metre part of the beach for your beach clean.

How to give a talk

It is really important to give a talk before everyone starts cleaning. Here are some things you should say:

- Introduce yourself.
- Talk about the problem of plastic litter on beaches and in

the ocean. Say why it is important to write down what litter you find. If you have done a beach clean before, talk about what you found and give any interesting statistics about your beach.

- Tell them if there is anything dangerous on the beach.
- Explain the survey form and how to use it.
- You could have a competition. The winner is the person who collects the most things, not the person who collects the heaviest things.
- Ask everyone if they are happy for you to take photos and post them online.
- Give them a time and place to meet again at the end.

During the beach clean

- What types of litter have people found? They need to tick the correct word on the survey form, for example wet wipe or cotton bud. Help them if they do not know what to tick.
- If you have a First Aid Kit and a container for collecting glass etc., keep it with you. Someone might need it.
- Take photos and share your experience online.

After the beach clean

- Weigh and count the bin bags. Count how many people helped you with the beach clean.
- Ask if anybody found anything interesting.
- What were most of the things they found (most of it was probably plastic)?
- Thank them for their help.

Leave the litter in the correct place and complete the first page of the survey form. Then, share it with MCS or a plastic campaign group in your area.

Back at home
Have a rest and tell yourself "Well done!" Share photos and stories about your day online. Send everyone a message to say, "Thanks for helping today!" and ask them to share their experience online, too.

#BreakFreeFromPlastic

Who are you?
Catherine Gemmell. I work for the Marine Conservation Society in Scotland.
Why do you care about plastic so much?
In my job for the Marine Conservation Society, I help thousands of amazing people in Scotland to collect plastic waste on their beaches. In the litter surveys that they do, I can see that most of what they collect is plastic.
What's the worst example of plastic pollution you've seen?
It only takes one plastic product to end the life of a beautiful sea animal, for example a turtle, and that breaks my heart. Some beaches are completely covered in plastic.

What's the best solution to the problem of plastic?

There is no easy solution to reducing plastic in our seas. It takes a lot of work from everyone, including people like us, businesses and government. There is a fantastic example from the UK, where lots of people and groups all worked together and, thanks to them, shoppers now have to pay 5p for each plastic bag. Within one year, there were 40% fewer plastic bags on our beaches, which shows how much we can achieve. It is great that the whole world knows that there is a problem with plastic and we all want change – politicians must listen to us and take action.

What changes have you made in your life to use less plastic?

I now use a wooden toothbrush instead of plastic, solid shampoo instead of liquid in bottles and deodorant bars. I also carry a KeepCup coffee cup, a metal water bottle and several reusable bags, as well as my own little cutlery. I am very proud that my family and friends are now trying to reduce their plastic use, too, and sometimes they do better than me!

What makes you most angry?

I do my best to reduce plastics, but then sometimes I find a plastic bag inside a cardboard box or a book arrives in the post that is wrapped in lots of plastic. That makes me very angry! It is difficult to reduce plastic but producers and sellers must join us and get rid of plastic in their products where it is possible.

Do you have any top tips for getting rid of plastic?
Get ideas from other people online. Social media is a great place for ideas – other people can give you tips for the best shops or websites, as well as blogs. The online plastic-free community is growing all the time and I encourage everyone to join it.

What makes it difficult to get rid of plastic?
What makes it difficult is how we make packaging – nothing should be thrown away. Companies that make plastic will have to make big, brave changes. The time is now!

"

Starting your own campaign

You have cleaned your beach and joined your nearest plastic campaign group, but maybe you want to do more! Why not run a campaign in your community about one of the products or plastic problems in this book? Here are a couple of ideas:

1. Bans on single-use plastic. Think about the plastic on your streets – who can stop it? You could encourage a café near your house to get rid of straws or the politicians for your area to ban plastic food containers and plastic cutlery in takeaway restaurants.

2. More water fountains. Tell businesses and politicians in your area that they should build more water fountains.

What problem are you trying to change? Write it down in fifty words or fewer.
What change needs to be made to help with the problem? Write it down in fifty words or fewer.

Now decide who you need to speak to. Who can make this change happen? Is it the director of a business or the government in your area? If you are not sure who to talk to, choose the most important person.

Write down the name of the person or people you are going to talk to about your campaign. This person or group of people is called your "target".

Now you just need a plan of action. Start with the smallest action, then each action should get bigger and bigger. Even if you feel angry, always be polite with people – you need their help and you are going to work together with them in the future.

On the next page is one possible plan of action that is like a ladder, so start at the bottom and go up. There is more information for each step on the following pages. You may have to repeat some steps. It is OK if your plan of action is different. Read about other people's campaigns to get ideas.

Letter writing

Writing letters or emails is one of the best ways to reach the right people. Someone will read your letter or email and that person might make the change that you want.

Introduction to writing a good letter

You have to write a good letter if you want to encourage someone to help you in your campaign. A letter written to the right person in your own voice is better than a copy of a letter from the internet. Follow these tips.

Be clear

What are the most important things that you need to say? What exactly are you asking the person to do and why?

Before starting your letter, answer the following questions using just one sentence:

1. What are you asking?

Are you asking the person to reduce their plastic footprint or stop selling a product? Do not ask them to help with too many things – two things are enough. Explain what you want them to do in the first paragraph of your letter.

2. Why are you asking for this?

In the next part of the letter, write about your own experiences and use examples or statistics to explain why you are asking them to reduce plastic pollution. Keep this part quite short.

3. What do you want the person to do?

Be friendly and positive in your letter. Be very clear and tell them what they need to do.

Keep it short

The person you are writing to is probably very busy so keep your letter short. One side of paper is enough. Try to use only one or two statistics or examples, choosing the best ones. If there is an interesting newspaper story that you want the person to read, do not write about it in your letter. Instead, include a copy of it or a **link** for them to read later.

Be personal

Statistics are very important, and they get people's attention, but you must also write about yourself – who are you and why does plastic pollution matter to you? Be personal – in other words, talk about your own experiences – because then your reader will be more interested in you and in your campaign. If you are a customer at their shop, tell them. Have you seen a bird taking pieces of plastic for its baby to eat? Does your favourite beach have lots of plastic litter on it? Tell them about it.

Be personal because then your reader will be more interested in you and in your campaign.

Be honest

After you have finished your letter, read it again carefully. Correct your grammar and spelling (or ask a friend to help you). Is everything you have said true? Do not say, "Thirteen million tonnes of plastic waste enter the ocean every year" if the true number is only 12.7 million. If you do that, your reader will not trust you and then they may not help you.

Be polite

Finally, remember to be polite. Would you reply to a rude letter, or would you reply to a letter that encouraged you? Also, do not forget to use formal language.

And that is all. If you follow these tips, you will be able to write a good campaign letter. Now, click "send" or post it. If you would like more tips, see the letter on the next page.

Dear Mrs Wan,

*What are
you asking?*

I am writing to you about the need for
more water fountains in the park on my
street. Over the past few years, I have

*Why are
you writing?*

noticed that the amount of plastic in the
park has increased a lot. Although there
are some bins, they are often too full and
the plastic falls out of the top, leaving litter
everywhere. A water fountain would
stop this.

I see plastic bottles all over the park.
These bottles pollute our beaches and
oceans. The plastic in our park could
enter the ocean if the wind takes it there.

*Interesting
statistic*

A plastic bottle can take over 400 years
to break down. Across the world, the
problem of plastic pollution is getting
bigger and bigger. For example, one
million plastic bottles are bought around
the world every minute. We must change
this to protect the ocean.

People should carry a reusable bottle
instead of using plastic bottles. If we
had water fountains in the park, it would

Examples

encourage more people to carry their own bottle because they could refill it at the fountain. The Zoological Society of London and Selfridges are two examples of large businesses that have completely stopped selling plastic bottles by buying more water fountains. They found that the water fountains led to 65% fewer water bottles. You could do the same in our park.

Make it personal

I love the park and I find it sad to see plastic in every part of it. It makes our community look untidy and it makes us look like we do not care about where we live. I would be very pleased if you would

What would you like the reader to do?

put water fountains in the park as soon as possible. I would be happy to meet you to discuss this more. Please write to me at the address given or you can call me on XXXXXXXXXXX.

Yours sincerely,

Will McCallum

Meeting

You may want to write a letter first and then go to a meeting or you could meet your target straight away, if you know them already. It is very important to meet the person whose help you need (see note on page 4). A good meeting can make someone take action. You can have one meeting or many.

Why do you need a meeting if you can give someone all the information in a letter? The difference is you and your story. When you meet someone, the way that you act can encourage them to help you. They can see that you are not very different from them – you are just an ordinary person who cares about something and who can talk politely about it.

How to prepare for a meeting

Write down the most important things you want to say: keep it short, clear, personal and honest, like in your letter. If you are nervous, practise a few times first. Write down a few statistics you want to use and ask a friend or parent to come with you. If they want to speak, too, decide who will say which part.

What will you take to the meeting? If you want the person to read a report that has all the important information in it, then take a copy of that report with you. Do you want them to sell reusable cups? Then take a reusable cup with you to show them. Have you found any of the company's products on the beach or in the park? Take photos and show them.

How to have a meeting

The most important thing is to leave the meeting with a new friend, someone who will help you to reduce plastics. You might be angry with them but, at least in the first meeting, stay polite. If a friend or parent is going with you, ask them to take notes during the meeting. You might not remember what was said.

When you talk, start and finish by saying exactly what you want the person to do. Ask them what they think of your idea and if they have any questions. Promise to write a letter or email, repeating what you want from them.

Many campaigns need several meetings so do not worry if you do not achieve everything in your first meeting.

The most important thing is to leave the meeting with a new friend, someone who will help you to reduce plastics.

Using the media

If you start a campaign in your community, it will be interesting to your city or area's newspaper, or radio or TV station. It is a journalist's job to find interesting stories, so they will be pleased to listen to you.

How to get their attention

First, write a press release: what is your news, why does it matter and who can people contact for more information?

Give your press release an exciting title, for example: "Businesses in our area throw away 100,000 coffee cups a year". Do not write too much and use only the best statistics, explaining the problem quickly. If your press release is about a future event, give the most important information about the event. Then say why this news is important and what you are asking for.

Another way to get attention is to use photos, so put some in the press release or make an online group of photos on Flickr and put a link in your press release.

Read your press release at least twice when you have finished it to check for mistakes. Get a friend or parent to read it, too. Have you used paragraphs well and are your spelling and grammar correct?

After you have sent the press release, call the journalist. Practise what to say first and have your press release with you when you call.

On the next page is an example of a press release.

Exciting title

Greenpeace report shows plastic footprint of world's largest fizzy-drinks companies

Quickly explain the story

Greenpeace UK has done a survey on the plastic footprint of the world's top six soft-drinks companies: Coca-Cola, PepsiCo, Suntory, Danone, Dr Pepper Snapple and Nestlé.

Despite plastic bottles being a large part of ocean plastic pollution, the survey shows that these companies are not doing enough to help.

Most important information

Important information:

- Of the six companies in the survey, five sell a total of **two million tonnes of plastic bottles a year**.

Best statistics

- The six companies use **only 6.6% recycled plastic** in their bottles.

- Over the past ten years, these companies have sold **fewer refillable bottles and more single-use bottles**.

- Two-thirds of the companies **do not want to introduce a deposit scheme**. This type of scheme has increased recycling in Germany by more than 98%.

Note to journalists:

A link to your photos

Photos of ocean plastic pollution can be found here: http://XXXXXXXXXXXX.

Contact information

For more information and **interviews**, contact: Luke Massey.

It is wonderful to see your story in a newspaper or hear it on the radio. But journalists are busy, so if they do not reply you can use social media instead. You could contact the same journalist on Twitter and tell them about your press release.

Starting a petition

Starting a petition is very easy. There are lots of online campaign groups to help you make and share a petition: Change.org, Avaaz or 38 Degrees, for example. Go to one of these websites and follow the steps.

Collect names

Post your petition on social media and email it to your

friends and family. Ask everyone to share it with *their* friends and family. Try to get 200 people to sign your petition.

Send your petition

When you have enough people on your petition, give it to the manager of the café or the politician, etc. (your "target"). Tell a journalist that you are giving it to your target – they might come and take photos of you! If the target still does not give you a meeting, then follow the next step.

Start a protest

When you think of a protest, you probably think of thousands of angry people walking together through the streets, loudly shouting their message. Of course, you can do that but it is not the type of protest I am talking about in this book. I am talking about getting your target's attention and making them listen. There are many examples of this type of protest. Here are just a few:

1. Take photos and share them. One of the simplest ways to get attention for your campaign is to show everyone what your target is doing wrong. If you want to reduce the use of plastic straws, ask friends to take a photo every time they see a straw littering the ground. Tag your target company in your social-media posts with the photo and ask them why they are not doing anything to help you. Companies do not like bad things written about them, so this may make them listen to you.

2. Send your target things. Ask people from your

petition to make something for your target. This could be a little fish made from paper or a glass container with the plastic rubbish they collected in it. These things are fun but your target probably does not want to receive hundreds of them, so it will make them listen to you and take action.

3. Online action. Ask everyone from your petition to send the company a message on Twitter or Facebook. Or you can all call the company at the same time to complain.

4. Leave it in the shop. Lots of companies are not listening to us about plastic packaging, so why not unwrap the product after you pay for it, and politely leave the packaging in the shop?

5. Send it back. If you are too shy to leave the packaging in the shop, then post it back to the company that made it. Include a note about why you are sending it back and ask them to tell you when they have recycled it.

Campaigning is fun but also tiring, so start with one small action and get bigger. For example, start with one café and then, later, all the cafés in your area. As you get more experience, you will learn how to encourage people, businesses and politicians to change.

Campaigning is fun but also tiring, so start with one small action and get bigger.

What about the future?

How to give up plastic – that was the promise of this book. The answer is by working together. We can do things alone and our actions are important but we can make a much bigger difference together. Sitting at home and worrying about the problem will not help. We must all take action now and ask companies and politicians to take action as well.

There is not one single way to give up plastic. It is different for every community and in every country. But there is one single message: we need to stop producing so much plastic. Plastic pollution should belong to the past.

Plastic is damaging the world's oceans, the world's animals and our health. Also, it is often the poorest people in the world who are affected most negatively by plastic pollution. We know that, and we know that we must get rid of plastic. Modern technology helps us to share this message with other people and this book gives you lots of ideas.

As you start getting rid of plastic in your life and community, remember to use your voice. Tell your friends about plastic pollution, tell the shops in your area and tell the newspapers. Plastic is not going to disappear in one day and it will not be easy. Millions more people must join us and you can help by sharing your story. Together, we can make a better world.

During-reading questions

1 What did Will McCallum find in the water when he was on a ship in the Antarctic?
2 Why did Will McCallum write this book?

CHAPTER ONE

1 Where and when was the first ban on plastic bags?
2 What is a deposit scheme?
3 What makes Luke Massey angry?

CHAPTER TWO

1 How much plastic is already in the ocean?
2 About one-third of the plastic in the oceans comes from one thing. What is it?
3 What is the waste trade?

CHAPTER THREE

1 How long does a plastic bag take to break down?
2 What, according to Louise Edge, is the best thing that people can do to help?

CHAPTER FOUR

1 What are "the Big 4"?

CHAPTER FIVE

1 What are refillables? Why are they good for the environment?
2 How can you avoid buying products with microbeads in?

CHAPTER SIX

1 How can you reduce plastic when you are shopping for clothes?

CHAPTER SEVEN

1 What hashtag (#) should you use on social media when you are writing about reducing plastic?
2 Find five ways that you can reduce plastic when you are shopping for food.
3 Bonnie Wright says that we should complain to companies. What should we complain to them about and why?

CHAPTER EIGHT

1 What is the problem with using single-use coffee cups?

CHAPTER NINE

1 Find five ways that you can use less plastic if you have a party.

CHAPTER TEN

1 How can you help to reduce plastic at a place of study or work?

CHAPTER ELEVEN

1 What two examples of campaigns does Will McCallum give?
2 If you want to start your own campaign, what is the first step in the plan of action? What are the other four steps?
3 Why is it important to meet someone, if you want them to reduce plastic?

CHAPTER TWELVE

1 "How to give up plastic" – that was the promise of this book. What is the answer?

After-reading questions

1 Read your answer to "Before-reading question 1" again. Has your answer changed after reading this book?

2 What things have you already done to reduce your plastic use?

3 What things do you plan to do soon to reduce your plastic use?

4 When thinking about plastic use, what makes you angry?

5 Which chapter did you find most interesting and why?

6 Which fact or statistic did you find most surprising and why?

7 What is the biggest problem with plastic in your country or area?

8 Has your country introduced any plastic bans?

Exercises

INTRODUCTION

1 Complete these sentences with the correct word in your notebook.

break down	straws	give up	tiny	packaging
	pollution	reusable	-free	

1 This book helps you to ....*give up*......... plastic so you can have a plastic .... life.

2 Plastic .... is a problem for every country in the world.

3 .... pieces of plastic enter the ocean.

4 Single-use plastics include ...., which people use to drink with, and plastic ....

5 They take centuries to ....

6 For this reason, it is better to buy .... coffee cups, bags and containers.

CHAPTER ONE

2 **Match the questions with their answers in your notebook.**

Example: 1 – e

1 Why do you care about plastic so much?

a Companies that produce single-use plastic should have to pay money to the government.

2 What's the best solution to the problem of plastic?

b A man called Rob Greenfield went on to the streets in New York wearing every piece of plastic he used in a month.

3 What makes you most angry?

c Companies not taking more responsibility for the plastic they produce.

4 Do you have any top tips for getting rid of plastic?

d Use less plastic. Take your own bag when you shop. Recycle as much as you can.

5 What is the most amazing thing that somebody has done to reduce plastic?

e It makes me sad to see the effects of plastic pollution on animals.

CHAPTER TWO

3 Write the correct verb form, *present simple passive*, *present perfect passive* or *past simple passive*, in your notebook.

1 Around 105 billion plastic bottles ......*are made*......... (**make**) by Coca-Cola every year.
2 A few years ago, 38 billion pieces of plastic .... (**find**) on Henderson Island in the South Pacific, where no people live.
3 Around 360 million tonnes of plastic .... (**produce**) every year.
4 A few years ago, 500,000 pieces of plastic .... (**find**) in every square metre in a river in Manchester, UK.
5 Since 2016, plastic bags .... (**ban**) in Banjarmasin, Indonesia.
6 Only 5% of the plastic we produce .... (**recycle**).
7 It .... (**estimate**) that 90% of seabirds have plastic in their stomachs.

CHAPTER THREE

4 Complete these sentences in your notebook, using words from the box.

> companies   fish   problem   beach   day   seabirds
> waste   packaging   birds

I visited Freedom Island, a home for [1] ....*birds*........... in Manila Bay. The whole beach was covered in plastic [2]........... In the sea, I saw plastic [3]........... next to dead [4]........... and [5]........... It made me really sad. I cleaned the [6]........... but the next [7]..........., there was more plastic waste. I realized that plastic packaging is a big problem and that we need the help of big [8]........... like Nestlé and Unilever. They make the packaging, and they must help with the [9]...........

5 Complete these sentences with *may*, *should*, *can* or *must*, in your notebook. More than one answer may be possible.

1 The changes we make in our own lives ....*can*............ have a big effect on others, so you .... tell people what you are doing and why.

2 If they hear our stories about reducing our plastic use, politicians .... be encouraged to make changes, too.

3 Tell other people about plastic as much as you ....

4 Reusable products .... also save you money.

5 Companies .... not make bottles from plastic that cannot be recycled.

6 We .... reduce our use of bottled water because in many countries the water is safe, so you do not need to buy plastic water bottles!

CHAPTER SEVEN

6 In which room do you normally find these things? Put these words into three groups in your notebook.

snack   sponge   deodorant   shampoo
washing-up liquid   refillable container   razor

Kitchen	Bathroom	Both
snack		

87

7 **Complete these sentences with the correct words in your notebook.**

million	one-third	over	short	every	around
billion	tens of	several	than half		

1 ....*Tens of*......... millions of people around the world watched *Blue Planet II*.

2 In Lake Ontario, there are .... 1.1 million microbeads for .... square kilometre.

3 In Britain, we use thirty-five .... plastic bottles every day and less .... of those bottles are recycled.

4 Coca-Cola is the world's largest producer of plastic bottles, making 105 .... a year.

5 In Germany and Norway, ... 90% of plastic bottles are recycled.

6 A .... time after the microbeads ban, ... countries banned cotton buds with plastic in them.

7 More than .... of the plastic in the ocean comes from our clothes when we wash them.

8 Complete the phrasal verbs with the correct particle in your notebook.

1 Do you have any top tips for getting rid ....*of*............ plastic?

2 It takes 450 years for a plastic bottle to break .... in the ocean.

3 Do not buy single-use razors or razors you throw .... after a few uses.

4 Write .... the plastic-free products that you or your parents will buy.

5 The easiest way to give .... plastic coffee cups is to get a reusable cup.

6 Ask friends to help you wash .... after the party so that you do not need to use single-use cups, plates and cutlery.

7 Put .... a poster or send an email to everyone.

9 According to Will McCallum, what should you buy instead of the products on the left? Match the products in your notebook.

Example: 1 – c

1 clothes with microfibres
2 a takeaway
3 wet wipes
4 small bottles of shampoo, for shower gel, etc.
5 a sponge
6 bottles of fizzy drink

a a loofah
b refillables
c cotton or wool
d a soda maker

e cotton pads
f fresh food

CHAPTER TWELVE

10 **Write the correct words in your notebook.**

1 gabs Bangladesh was the first country to ban plastic
...............*bags*...............

2 cmior Scientists found .... plastics in every human
poo they tested.

3 efre Will you try a plastic-.................July?

4 awtes Birds feed plastic .... to their babies because
they think that the plastic is food.

5 reedyccl If you cannot find a drink in cardboard, a can
or a glass bottle and you cannot

ycerllbcae find a bottle made from .... plastic, then
at least choose one made from .... plastic.

6 ussngiele- Why do you use plastic cutlery and ....
coffee cups?

7 apgcaikng The whole beach was covered in plastic ....

Project work

1 Carefully plan one of these activities. What will you need?
What will you have to do? Who will you have to speak to?
- a beach clean
- a plastic-free party
- a plastic-free competition
- ask a plastics campaigner to give a talk

2 Write a letter to one of these people about reducing plastic. Use the advice and example letter in Chapter Eleven to help you.
   • the director of your school or university
   • the manager of your nearest takeaway restaurant, café, cinema, etc.
   • the politician for your area

Next, have a meeting with your chosen person. Take a parent or friend with you.

3 Write a press release about your meeting (question 2). Use the advice and example press release in Chapter Eleven to help you. Then call the journalist and talk to them.

4 Complete the plastic promise and the plastic-free plans in the book.

5 Research one of these topics and prepare a presentation.
   • Sisters Amy and Ella Meek, for example their website and TedX talk.
   • Chris Jordan and his photo of a dead baby albatross in the North Pacific.
   • The video of a plastic straw being taken out of a turtle's nose.
   • One of the plastic campaigns from the book.
   • A plastic campaign from your country or area.

Glossary

ban (v. and n.)
If a *government bans* something, it says that people must not use, sell or do it. *Ban* is the noun of *ban*.

bedding (n.)
Bedding covers you so that you stay warm in bed. It is made of *material*.

blame (v.)
to say that someone did
something wrong

blog (n.)
when someone writes their ideas
on the internet for people to read

break down (phr. v.)
If *plastic* or other *materials break
down*, they slowly go into very
small parts and then disappear.
It can take a very long time for
plastic to *break down*.

campaign (n. and v.)
when you plan and do several
activities because you want people
to make something happen or
change. *Campaign* is the verb of
campaign.

cardboard (n. and adj.)
very thick, strong paper. Boxes
and other *containers* are often
made of *cardboard*. *Cardboard* is
the adjective of *cardboard*.

cloth (n.)
Cloth is soft and flat and you use it
to make clothes, curtains, *bedding*
etc. A *cloth* is a piece of this and is
used to clean things, or cover them.

community (n.)
a group of people who all live in
the same place

complain (v.)
to say that you are not happy
about something

container (n.)
something that you can put other
things in. Boxes, bottles and bags
are *containers*.

decoration (n.)
Decorations are things that you put
on or around something so that it
looks nice or pretty.

deodorant (n.)
You put *deodorant* under your
arms to stop your body from
smelling bad.

disabled (adj.)
If someone is *disabled*, they have
a problem with their body which
makes it difficult for them to do the
things that other people can do.

discount (n.)
money which is taken from the
price of something so that it is
cheaper

drain (n.)
a hole or pipe (= a long, round
plastic or metal thing) that takes
dirty water or *waste* away from
a building

effect (n.)
a change that happens because of another thing

encourage (v.)
to say that someone should do something because you think it is the right thing for them to do

estimate (v.)
to say what you think an amount or time will be, either by guessing or using information to help you

First Aid Kit (n.)
a box or bag of things that you use to help a person who is suddenly hurt or ill

fizzy drink (n.)
a drink which has a lot of bubbles (= balls of gas) in it. *Fizzy drinks* are usually made with soda.

footprint (n.)
Your *footprint* is the amount of *pollution* or *waste* that comes from the things that you do or use.

fountain (n.)
a water *fountain* or drinks *fountain* is a machine that you drink water from in an office, school, park, etc. The *fountain* pushes the water up into the air so that you can put your mouth over it.

-free (suffix)
-free is used at the end of words to mean 'without'. For example, *plastic-free* means 'without *plastic*'.

get rid of (phr. v.)
to take something to another place because you do not want it with you any more

give up (phr. v.)
to stop using or doing something

government (n.)
a group of important people who decide what must happen in a country

interview (n.)
when someone asks a person a lot of questions to learn information about something

landfill site (n.)
A *landfill site* is a place where *waste* is put under the ground. If something *goes to landfill*, it is taken to a *landfill site*.

link (n.)
A *link* takes you to another area or document on the internet.

litter (n.)
pieces of paper, rubbish and other *waste* that people leave on the ground

make-up (n.)
special colours that you put
on your face to make you look
different or more beautiful

material (n.)
1) You use *materials* like *plastic*,
wood etc. to make things.
2) *Material* is soft and flat and
you use it to make clothes,
curtains, *bedding* etc. Another
word for *material* is *cloth*.

microbeads (n.)
very small balls of *plastic* that
you cannot see

nappy (n.)
a thick, soft piece of special
plastic or *cloth* that babies or very
young children wear on their
bottom to catch *waste* from
their bodies

packaging (n.)
boxes, bags, paper or *plastic*.
Food or other things that you
buy are often inside packaging.

pad (n.)
a piece of soft, thick special
plastic or *cloth* that you use to
stop things getting dirty or make
them more comfortable. You
can use small *pads* to take *make-up* off your face.

petition (n.)
A document that asks a
government, company or
other group of people to do
something. Many people write
their names on it. *Petitions* are
often used in *campaigns*.

plastic (n. and adj.)
plastic is strong and light. It is
made in factories and used to
make a lot of things that we use
every day, for example bags and
cups. *Plastic* is the adjective of
plastic.

politician (n.)
a person who works in the
government

pollution (n.); **pollute** (v.)
when air, water or land is
damaged by waste and becomes
dirty and dangerous for animals
or people. *Pollute* is the verb of
pollution.

poo (n.)
solid waste from your body

poster (n.)
a large piece of paper which has
a picture or writing on it. You
put it on a wall, often because
you want to tell people about
something.

powder (n.)
something like sugar or sand that is soft and dry, and made of very small pieces. You use tooth *powder* to clean your teeth.

product (n.); **produce** (v.)
Products are the many things that companies make to sell. People buy and use lots of different *products*. If companies *produce* things, they make these things so that they can sell them.

recycle (v.)
to do something to *plastic*, paper or glass so that you can use them again

reduce (v.)
to make something less or smaller

refill (v.); **refillable** (n. and adj.)
If you *refill* a *container*, it is empty and you fill it with something again. If a *container* is *refillable*, you can fill it with something again. A *refillable* is a *container* that you can *refill* many times.

responsibility (n.)
something that people should or must do. If you take *responsibility* for something, often something bad, you say that you have done it or made it happen.

reusable (adj.)
You can use a *reusable* thing again and again.

shampoo (n.)
ou use *shampoo* with water to wash your hair.

shower gel (n.)
You use *shower gel* to wash your body in the shower.

snack (n.)
a small amount of food that you eat between meals

soap (n.)
You use *soap* with water to wash yourself or clean things.

solid (adj.)
hard like rock and not liquid (= a thing like water) or gas

solution (n.)
an answer to a question or problem

sponge (n.)
a *sponge* is soft and has a lot of small holes that water goes into. You use it to wash yourself or clean things.

statistics (n.)
numbers that show information about something

straw (n.)
a long thin piece of *plastic* or paper. You put it in a glass and drink with it.

survey (n.)
a group of questions that you ask a lot of people. You do a *survey* to collect information about what people do or think.

tag (v.)
If you *tag* someone in a photo on social media (= websites like Facebook, Instagram, or Twitter), you add a *link* to a place on the internet which has information about them.

tampon (n.)
a special kind of *pad* that a woman puts inside her to catch the blood that comes out of her body every month

tide (n.)
when the sea moves towards land and away from it every day

tiny (adj.)
extremely small

tip (n.)
a small piece of advice

tonne (n.)
1000 kilograms

toothpaste (n.)
You use *toothpaste* to clean your teeth.

turtle (n.)
an animal with four legs and a hard cover on its back. *Turtles* usually live in the sea.

waste (n.)
things that you do not want. *Waste* is often what is there after you have used something.

wet wipe (n.)
a small, soft, wet piece of special *plastic* or *cloth* that you use to clean your body or other things.

wrap (v. and n.); **unwrap** (v.); **wrapping paper** (n.)
If you *wrap* something, you put paper, *material*, *plastic*, etc around it to cover it. If you *unwrap* something, you take the paper, *material*, *plastic*, etc away so that it is not covered. *Wrapping paper* is often used to *wrap* presents. *Plastic wrap* is sometimes used to *wrap* food.